Bel Mooney   Margaret Chamberlain

Mr. Tubs
is
LOST!

Blue Bananas

Crabtree Publishing Company
www.crabtreebooks.com

PMB 16A, 350 Fifth Avenue,
Suite 3308,
New York, NY 10118

616 Welland Avenue,
St. Catharines, Ontario
Canada, L2M 5V6

For Sophie Rose Evans
B.M.

For Anne Veronica
M.C.

Mooney, Bel, 1946-
    Mr. Tubs is lost! / written by Bel Mooney ; illustrated by Margaret Chamberlain.
       p. cm. -- (Blue bananas)
    Summary: Accidentally left in the woods by his owner, Mr. Tubs the teddy
bear meets many woodland creatures, some who are kind and some who are scary.
    ISBN-13: 978-0-7787-0858-2 (rlb) -- ISBN-10: 0-7787-0858-6 (rlb)
    ISBN-13: 978-0-7787-0904-6 (pbk) -- ISBN-10: 0-7787-0904-3 (pbk)
    [1. Teddy bears--Fiction. 2. Lost and found possessions--Fiction. 3. Forest
animals--Fiction.] I. Chamberlain, Margaret, ill. II. Title. III. Series.
    PZ7.M779Mrt 2006
    [E]--dc22
                                                                2005035766
                                                                   LC

Published by Crabtree Publishing in 2006
First published in 2004 by Egmont Books Ltd.
Text copyright © Bel Mooney 2004
Illustrations copyright © Margaret Chamberlain 2004
The Author and Illustrator have asserted their moral rights.
Paperback ISBN 0-7787-0904-3
Reinforced Hardcover Binding ISBN 0-7787-0858-6

"TEDDY BEARS PICNIC" Words by Jimmy Kennedy and
Music by John W Bratton © 1932, M Witmark & Sons, USA
Reproduced by permission of B Feldman & Co Ltd, London WC2H 0QY.

Mr. Tubs's favorite song

If you go down to the woods today
You're sure of a big surprise.
If you go down to the woods today
You'd better go in disguise.
For every bear that ever there was
Will gather there for certain because
Today's the day the teddy bears have their picnic!

Mr. Tubs liked to go everywhere with Kitty. He knew she needed him to look after her.

Mr. Tubs knew that Kitty was

always losing her things.

But he knew where everything was.

Some days Kitty even lost Mr. Tubs!

She'd race around the house yelling,

"Mr. Tubs, where are you?"

I'm over here, Kitty!

All he could do was just lie there and

wait to be found.

Then Kitty would cuddle him and whisper, "Promise you'll never run away again, Mr. Tubs, because I'd miss you sooooooo much!"

When Kitty got into trouble he tried to help her. But sometimes Kitty was too busy (or angry) to hear him.

One sunny day Mom and Dad told Daniel and Kitty they were all going to the woods for a picnic. Mom was already making sandwiches.

"Can we have peanut butter?" Kitty asked. "It's Mr. Tubs's favorite."

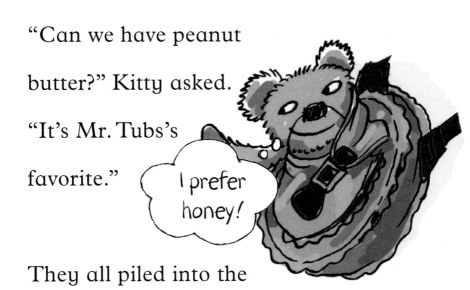

They all piled into the car. Mr. Tubs sat on Kitty's knee. As the trees sped by he felt very cheerful.

Kitty sang Mr. Tubs's favorite song at the top of her voice, and the others joined in. It was true – he did like going down to the woods.

Today's the day the teddy

bears have their picnic!

Come on, Team!

When they got to the woods, Dad gave each person a job. He took the heavy picnic backpack.

13

Mom carried the cooler
bag and her basket.

Dan carried

the blanket.

Kitty carried a baseball
bat and a red ball.
Mr. Tubs held on to
Kitty's arm, just in
case she got lost.

It was a beautiful day. The woods
looked magical. As they walked
to their favorite spot Mr. Tubs
dreamed of real bears, waving to
him from the bushes.

The birds sang, the leaves rustled, and
Mr. Tubs felt very happy. He sat under a
tree and watched his family play baseball.
"You can keep score, Mr. Tubs" Kitty
called – and so he did.

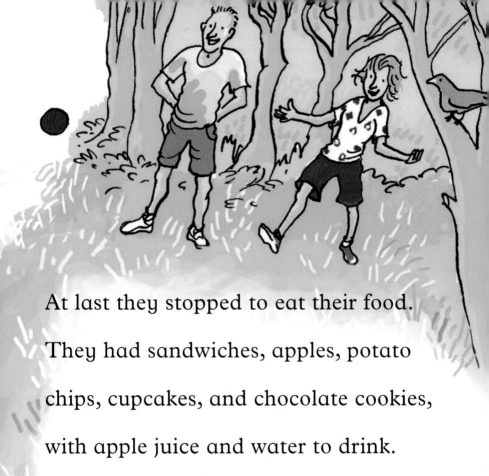

At last they stopped to eat their food.

They had sandwiches, apples, potato

chips, cupcakes, and chocolate cookies,

with apple juice and water to drink.

Everything was perfect, until . . .

. . . Kitty got **angry**.

"You took the last peanut butter sandwich, Dan!" she yelled. "It's not fair!"

"Kitty's so gree–eedy," teased her brother in a sing song voice, making her angrier than ever.

That's mine!

Please give it to her, Dan!

She jumped up and chased him
around the clearing, but he danced
in front of her, always out of reach,
waving the last sandwich.

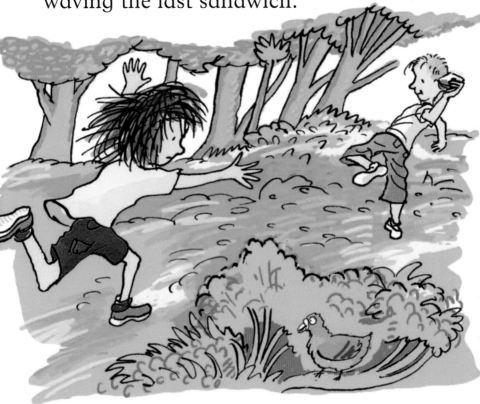

Mom and Dad told them to stop but
they took no notice.

Kitty stumbled over the edge of the blanket, and fell against the picnic backpack, knocking it over. Luckily she didn't hurt herself but she did kick over Mom's basket, scattering her purse, some tissues, a comb, and a bag of candy.

Oh, no!

Very angry, Mom jumped up,
shouting, "Oh, Kitty!"
Mom didn't notice that she'd
accidentally caught poor old
Mr. Tubs with her heel and rolled
him over backwards, so he was
hidden under a bush.

"It's all Dan's fault," wailed Kitty.

"Your fault for being greedy," muttered Dan.

It's not Kitty's fault!

Dad sighed and said, "Why is it that you kids spoil things? Come on, I think we should pack up and go home."

Time to go.

Mr. Tubs lay behind the leaves. He could just see his family packing up, and waited for Kitty to come and find him.

But Kitty was still hot and angry. She was unhappy too, because she knew she shouldn't have chased Dan.

She wanted to say "I'm sorry" to Mom, but the words got stuck.

It didn't take long to pack up. Soon they were ready to leave. All Kitty could think about was how bad she felt. The others were sad the day was spoiled. Nobody remembered Mr. Tubs. They began to walk back to the car.

Mr. Tubs heard their soft footsteps
getting fainter and fainter.

Coo!

Then suddenly all he could
hear was the song of the birds.
An ant ran over his nose.
Mr. Tubs felt very alone.

Tweet!

He lay there, waiting for Kitty to

come running back through the trees.

He knew she couldn't go to sleep

without him, and felt very worried.

A fly landed on his ear.

Mr. Tubs thought he heard it buzzing,

"Nobody wantzzzz you,

Mr. Tubszzzzzz."

Many hours passed.

The afternoon got smaller

and smaller as the evening

came, and Mr. Tubs's little

furry heart got smaller and

smaller too.

Help!

Suddenly the sun wasn't there any more. The shadows grew long.

Mr. Tubs thought about Kitty, as if wishing would make her come back. But she didn't.

Kitty will be having her dinner now.

It was darker now. Mr. Tubs
saw the first star through the
leaves. Then he heard a
rustling and felt afraid.

But when he saw the little rabbit
twitching its nose, he smiled. Bears
aren't afraid of rabbits,
after all.

Time passed. There was a snuffling
sound near his head. What could it
be? Mr. Tubs wanted to shout "Go
away!" but he couldn't.

When he saw the sharp eyes of the fox he was very scared. But the fox knew a teddy bear wouldn't be good to eat and went on his way. He was looking for the rabbit . . .

The next animal to come along was a small deer. She peered under the bush with her soft brown eyes. Her breath was warm.

Mr. Tubs was sure he heard her whisper, "Are you lost, little bear?" She seemed so gentle he wished he could go with her.

In the tree above, the owl cried,

"Whoooo . . . loooost . . . yoooooou?"

Suddenly the deer danced away.

Something had frightened her.

To Mr. Tubs's horror, a snake slithered up to his head. Her eyes glittered like little black buttons.

"Sssssssilly sssssssoft Tubsssssss," she hissed, but didn't stop long enough to let him growl

He would have frightened her right back,

that's for sure.

Kitty always said she didn't like snakes,

and he knew he had to look after her.

Oh . . . but he forgot. Kitty wasn't there.

Mr. Tubs felt something tickle his ear.

A tiny vole had crept up to him and snuggled by his head to keep warm. This was such a nice feeling it reminded Mr. Tubs of being in bed with Kitty. That made him very sad.

Go to sleep, little vole.

Suddenly two sets of eyes gleamed in the darkness. Mr. Tubs felt the little vole shiver. Knowing he had to look after him, he glared back at the scary eyes and sent his biggest, deepest growl rumbling through the gloom.

GRRRRR!

The two weasels yipped in terror and scampered away.

Oh, thank you, Mr. Tubs!

Now Mr. Tubs felt very brave. I may be little, but I'm being a real bear, he thought. He knew that if there were any big bears in that wood (and who knows? There might be . . .) they'd take him with them as one of the gang.

Time to go home, Mr. Tubsy.

Suddenly there was a rumble and a crash. Something big was coming. Mr. Tubs thought about those real bears and gulped. What if they didn't like little bears who smelt of human cuddles? But the animal looking at him now had a big snout and a black and white face.

The little vole ran away with a tiny squeak.

Help!

It was a badger!

But the badger didn't stay long. He lumbered away at the sudden sound of footsteps. The bright beam of a flashlight made a path through the darkness of the woods.

Mr. Tubs heard a voice
say, "Where were we today?
I think it was here . . ."
Then his heart went
pitter-patter.

. . . and there was Mr. Tubs.
Dad swept him up with
a whoop of joy.

Back home, Dad
crept into the house
and up the stairs.
Kitty was in bed.

She had been crying. Dan and Mom were trying to comfort her. "I want Mr. Tubs," sniffed Kitty. "He'll be cold out there."

"Don't worry, sweetie, I know Dad will find your bear," said Mom.

Mr. Tubs!

"Of course he will," said Daniel.

Just then Dad ran into the room,

waving Mr. Tubs in the air.

Kitty snuggled down with her bear.

"But you promised me you'd be good and not run away," she whispered.

Mr. Tubs wanted to tell her she'd got it wrong. It was Kitty who had lost him!

But he knew he'd just have to look after her a bit better from now on.